SUPER USELESS

JM LEWIS

ISBN 979-8-9996298-0-7 (paperback)
ISBN 979-8-9996298-1-4 (digital)

Hobo Shack Publishing www.originalhoboshack@gmail.com

Printed in the United Staes of America.

This book is dedicated to Kelik, Aveon, Kianna, Braalon, Daniel Jr, Davien, Kordell, Kyree, Alexa, Keaton, Carter, Jaez'lyn, Kaylecia, and all of my cousins. Laugh every day, focus on the positive, and be helpful wherever you're at.

SUPER USELESS

JM LEWIS

CONTENTS

PROLOGUE

Standing naked with my teammates huddled around me, using their hands to shield their eyes from the view of my... *goods*... is actually pretty much the norm for me.

The name's Jeffery. I'm calculated and cunning in a way that's intimidating to many. And not just because of my lack of clothing. My sharp mind and quick wit makes me an excellent planner—usually.

But I'm only like this when I'm naked.

"All right, break!" I holler, and the team joins in, and the group breaks apart. I throw on the balled-up trench coat by my feet to cover myself up, and the second I've tied the knot, everything changes. And it's a drastic change.

"H-hey, guys—d-did ya ever hear that joke about the m-monkey and the bank-robbing lizard?" I ask the group, who all roll their eyes and groan and mutter things like, "Not now, Jeffrey."

I mean, they're right. I should focus.

Because right now, inside the very bank we're standing in the alley of, three masked robbers are holding hostages at gunpoint and stuffing cash in the bags. No alarms were triggered.

Apparently, the robbers covered everything.

Dejuan quickly digs in his fanny pack and pulls out a chicken wing dripping with barbecue sauce. He quickly holds it out to the squealing little Japanese girl in front of him. "Are you kidding me, Dejuan?!" she yells, stifling a gag, turning slightly green in the face. "You *know* I hate barbecue sauce!"

Dejuan pushes his glasses up on his nose and shrugs. "It was all I could find last minute.

Sorry!"

I start feeling a little bit nervous as I look around at everyone. We don't have the whole team with us. Some are still back at headquarters or at work. Can we really do this?

"Uh, guys, not to be a pain, but we really should get going." I turn to Ainsley, the forced alcoholic. "You, um, are you ready, Ainsley?"

He looks sort of like this is boring him and downs a bottle of alcohol, right there in the alleyway. The whole thing. All down his gullet at a pretty speedy pace. Once it's done, he drops it to the floor and wobbles in place. But I know that means he's ready now.

My stomach dips nervously, still afraid that we won't actually pull this off. Near Ainsley, Borbola stands with ripping muscles, but holding her crotch and slightly bouncing up and down.

Par for the course. She only gets those ripping biceps of hers if she has to pee.

I slowly turn back to Koemi, hoping she's gotten over her barbecue sauce fear and downed the damn chicken wing. Thankfully, she's plugging her nose and in the middle of going to town on it, glaring at Dejuan.

It's time.

"Go! Go! Go!" I shout to Ainsley.

Ainsley finishes chugging one more can of high-alcohol-content beer, crushes it, and then ungracefully gets down into a track sprinter pose. I gotta admit, even sloppy and drunk, that's one good-looking dude. Some guys get all the luck.

Ainsley wobbles some more. "Let's give these wankers a proper wake-up call." *Hiccup.* "Crack on then. The Speed Demon has work to do." *Hiccup.*

And then he takes off, moving at the speed of a fast car. As though he's the drunk driver of one; he crashes into multiple cars and buildings before he manages to make it inside the building.

Dejuan shakes his head. "At least he's only the distraction."

I hear a squawk. Koemi now has chicken wings for arms and a beak-like mouth.

"Right!" *Cluck cluck.* "I'm ready." She flaps and struggles to lift off.

"Hey, Jeff? Can chickens even fly?" Dejuan asks.

"Kind of... I think."

Thankfully, she gets high enough off the ground for Borbola to grab onto her ankles and dangle below. Those two take off down the alley next. Koemi's got no control. Never been a great flier. She and Borbola are slamming into everything on their way. And Borbola? Her stoic, unimpressed face doesn't change. No matter what they hit.

Even from a distance, when I make out the sound of Koemi's stomach starting to rumble, my chest tightens. I'm beginning to think this might not go as planned.

"Who else is out here?!" an angry voice yells.

"Hurry up and shoot that fast one!" another yells.

"Oi! You shoot like my nan!" I hear Ainsley, but I don't see him.

Ainsley blurs around them with super speed, then grabs one robber who flails in fear.

Oh, this isn't happening right now! He's not supposed to grab them, just distract them!

BAM!

Ainsley crashes into a light pole. He falls to the ground and does not move. But the momentum he'd been carrying continues through the masked robber he'd been holding, who then goes flying towards a wall—*that's gonna hu—* **SPLAT!**

He slams hard into the wall. Dollar bills from his bag burst into the air.

I squint at the sound of retching. It's Koemi—she vomits midair, and it splatters across Borbola's still-apathetic face. She grunts; she can't see anything now. The two of them haven't even reached the bank yet.

Yeah. I'm definitely losing hope here.

I turn to Dejuan. "Remember, don't activate until—"

POOF!

It's too late.

Dejuan's dark skin turns neon green and starts to bubble up. It then puffs out, and before I know it, he's fully turned into a neon green blob.

"Sorry, you know it activates when I'm nervous." He pushes his glasses up again— somehow, they managed to stay on during his transformation. It's really the only recognizable part about him now.

I sigh and begin rolling Dejuan down the alley—we'll need him and his blubbery protectiveness to save the hostages. But as we roll down the street, everything sticks to him. Mainly trash, but then some heavier things like a discarded car tire and crumbled bits of brick wall that broke off when the robber slammed into it. Even the dang bank's dumpster. Dejuan gets heavier and heavier as the items glue to him, making it more of a challenge for gawky, lanky me to push and roll him.

The other two robbers avoid the large green man and dart over to their guy on the wall.

"He—he's dead!" one calls.

"Crap!" the other rumbles. "Someone's gonna pay for this!" They turn their guns to Ainsley, who is still unconscious on the ground. Thankfully, this is when Remy runs up out of nowhere, his red curly hair blowing in the breeze, his hands firm on his hips—classic superhero stance. I'd roll my eyes at him if I wasn't so desperate for his powers to actually help us this time.

"How you say—*freeze*! Le dirty scoundrels!" Remy's face turns red and scrunches up with anger—typical of him in most situations—and he activates his power and calls upon the help of...

Insects.

Yep. Bugs.

The robbers turn their guns at Remy and start blasting. Creepy crawlies intercept the bullets and sacrifice themselves for their arrogant overlord. Borbola finally drops from the still dry-heaving, uncontrollable, flying Koemi right down onto the robbers. Koemi, freed of the huge, muscular crutch, flaps off behind a dumpster—it doesn't ever just come out one way, if you know what I mean.

Borbola, still blinded from the foul-smelling puke, knocks the guns out of the robbers' hands, but not before a few shots are fired. One bullet ricochets off of the light post and hits Borbola in her massively strong arm. It doesn't affect her physically, but mentally, she finally changes her facial expression—she's freaked. Swearing in Russian, she swings her massive, strong arms blindly. Unsure of what or who she's hitting, her strong fists slam through brick walls and cars and knock down light poles. And when her pinky accidentally grazes Remy, it sends him flying down the alley.

It's a bit distracting to hear the unfathomable noises coming from behind the dumpster as Koemi's bowels erupt. "I'm sorry, guys," her voice squeaks out. It amazes me these violent sounds of explosive diarrhea can come out of such a small, innocent chick. "Can someone, please, hand me a few of those dollar bills?"

We're all a little busy though. The robbers try to duck Borbola's punches while reaching for their guns. I face-palm myself from behind Dejuan as she connects with one of the robbers and sends him to space. "It was such a good plan... in theory," I mutter to myself.

"Oh, screw this!" The last robber, all on his own, Borbola closing in, caves, turning and running off, dropping his bag of money before he goes.

I can hear the hostages freaking out and making a break for it, spilling out the bank doors as I round the corner with Dejuan. The hostages all run past us. "Wait, you can hide behind this green guy for protection!" They don't listen.

All goes silent.

I guess... at least the hostages are safe and far from the bank. It's over.

Dejuan shrinks back to normal. Koemi's hand comes out from behind the dumpster to pick up some loose, fluttering cash. We can all tell she's wiping her butt with it. When she returns, she's wiping her mouth and back to her normal form.

Borbola wipes Koemi's vomit from her face, her muscles still huge, which can only mean her bladder must be full to bursting by now. Ainsley slowly sits up, groaning, fixing his hair, just now coming to.

I look around at my team. This was a disaster.

Money is spewed about in the alley. Everything is destroyed. We only caught one bad guy, and it's because we accidentally killed him.

"I-I saw this going differently in my head," I tell the group.

Police sirens blare in the distance.

"BAH!" Remy hollers. "Deesaster!"

Koemi gasps and nervously covers her mouth with her hand. "Guys! Let's get out of here!"

"But I... I need to—" Borbola's pants darken at the crotch. A relieved look crosses over her. "Never mind." Her muscles shrink back to normal.

We make a break for it.

Super Useless

CHAPTER 1

I'm Jeffery Stints, the leader of the Super Useless team. Yep. You read that right. That's the name we've been given by news stations and media. Can you guess why?

The guys and I stay on the move, mainly because of the collateral damage we cause everywhere we go. Well, that—and... we've sort of also received a lot of death threats from the general public in recent months.

It's hard to be a hero and live a secret life without any actual training. If I am being honest, we usually get our ideas and tips from spy movies. James Bond. Bourne movies. Even Spy Kids and Johnny English.

Anyway, we stop crime, the best way we know how. We may not be great at it, but it's really the only life we know. I mean, most of us weren't popular in school, well, maybe Ainsley, and I'm not sure about Borbola. Nonetheless, the universe brought us together for a reason, right?

Currently, we're in the ole team bus. An ancient, gray blue Dodge Ram Passenger van. We picked the others up from HQ, along with a few essentials, and hit the road again. The nine of us are feeling pretty darn defeated. Borbala has piss stains on her spring dress, Koemi has dried vomit on the front of her pink, flowery Kawaii shirt, Dejaun's got an old banana peel stuck in his tightly coiled black hair.

"Well, it didn't take long in that town," Frankie grumbles in his Jersey accent.

"Always ze same. In any town," Remy snarkily says in response.

"We suck at being heroes," Koemi says with a sad sigh, dropping her head down.

We drive for hours. It's late into the night when we finally arrive at an old warehouse in a new state.

"We're home," Wekesa says in the saddest voice I've ever heard. His tone doesn't match his colorful attire and sassy manicure. I don't blame him. The new place Dejaun found for us— he's the techy guy out of all of us, in charge of hacking systems and finding us ways to live on the down low. The warehouse sits in the middle of a large plot of grass, hardly any trees around for miles. Just grassy plains all around, a dirt road leading up to it. The warehouse metal walls are patched up with rotting wood in many places. A rusty roof shows off its sagginess in the moonlight. The door hangs from one hinge.

Inside isn't any better. Sure, its' spacious, plenty of areas to hang our curtains and room

dividers, even an upstairs, so we can all have our own space. An office. A commercial grade bathroom with questionable plumbing. But old crates and boxes litter the space, take up room, and give it an odd smell.

Somberly, we unload wheelchair-bound Frankie and start setting up the team HQ inside the rotting space. The living area is also where our hero workspace/meeting space will be. Then we use whatever materials we can find so we all have our own makeshift rooms.

I rub my hands together as I set up my laptop on my desk—I'm the team leader, so I was given the only actual room in this place—what used to be a main office for someone. "Alright!" I call through my open door. Thankfully, this one has all its hinges, "First thing tomorrow, we all have to go out and find jobs! You know the drill."

I walk out to the main room. Remy makes a bench out of crates and boxes and is lounging lazily on it.

"Remy, come on, man." I motion to everyone else who is still working to carry in supplies from the van. Even Frankie is being more helpful than him.

Remy sits there on his phone, likely searching for mysterious caves or rumored hidden treasure locations nearby, before he finally gets to his feet. "I 'ate zis place. All of you, zis dump, zis... how you say... catastrophe! Pah! No respect. Of course not. And yet, who saved your sorry lives? *Moi!* With *my* superpower!!"

"Okay, Remy," I sigh. Wekesa shakes his head as he walks past with computer equipment. Barbola furrows her thick brows as she carries in a folding desk.

"Zat's right," Remy goes on, even though no one wants to hear it. "You know zomething, eef you sink for a second I wouldn't walk ze hell away if I had ze chance, you don't know me at all.." And with that, he storms outside.

I doubt he's gone out there to help unload, though. Moments later, we hear Remy's signature arguing. He's arguing with the insects—crickets specifically—but only he can hear what they are saying. To most people, it looks like Remy is arguing with himself.

"No! *You* are ze racist coward! What do I care eef you're black—*all* crickets are black! Eet's your *stupid* chirping zat pisses me off! What do you mean, you don't feel heard? I 'ave to leesten to your crap all night, every night!"

Inside, the team all roll their eyes and return to unpacking.

CHAPTER 2

"I thought we were only grabbing—" Trailer Park Trish pulls something out of a box in the living area of the warehouse— "the essentials." A pair of Wekesa's underwear, with the butt blown out, dangles in the air for everyone to see. Even Remy, who couldn't take anymore nagging crickets outside and came back in here.

He still didn't help, though.

"Gross! Wekesa!" Koemi cries, giggling slightly as her face scrunches up in disgust.

"Why do you keep those?"

"Because!" Wekesa barks in his strong African accent. "We never stay in one place long enough for me to work a job and be able to afford new underwear." He snatches them out of Trish's pudgy hands. "Plus, these are ready for me for when I need to activate my power."

"That's bloody rank," Ainsley says, shaking his head. He's on the couch again, picking at his own toenails.

"Shut up, *Anus-lee*," Wekesa says, putting a hand on his jutted-out hip. "Why don't you run along and continue bellowing about your hatred of us and your life. Go find that dream job of yours you want so bad."

"Wait, what *is* your dream job?" Koemi asks him.

Ainsley sits up, eager to talk about himself. "Why, being a model, of course. An actor if

I'm asked, I suppose. But I'd be willing to wager modeling is the easier gig."

There's a collective noise of groans and headshakes—except from Trish, whose eyes light up. She adjusts the feather boa around her neck, throwing the tail of one end over her very wide shoulder. "Oooh! I want to be a star too, Ainsley! But in reality TV. Or as an influencer.

That'd be so fun. My personality really shines, you know?"

Remy scoffs at her. "You? A reality TV star or influencer?" He spits with laughter.

Trish rolls her eyes. "It's only a matter of time before I have Hollywood calling me. You just wait and see."

"But... um... Trish?" Dejuan asks, sounding a bit cautious and confused as he gets the headquarters computers up and running. "Don't you only have... one follower?"

"Yeah, and it's her cousin!" Ainsley calls. "She's barking mad, I tell you!" He and Remy burst into laughter.

"Fine then, Remy," Trish says. "Why don't *you* go ahead and tell us what your dream job

is, then?"

"Isn't it obvious? With the metal detector he carries around everywhere he can?" Frankie asks. "The guy wants to be a freakin' pirate or somethin'."

"A *treasure hunter*, zank you very much," Remy corrects, his face reddening like usual.

Something with red hair and pale skin—an easily red face just seems to go hand in hand with it. "Ha!" Trish cries, pointing her fat finger at him. "That's not a real job!"

"Guys, don't fight!" Koemi pleads, stapling up some boyband posters to the walls of the living quarters.

"Is it *your* dream to be a groupie or something?" Borbola asks her, shaking her head disapprovingly at the posters. "Those... *boys* you worship. So little. They'd never be able to handle Borbola. *Pft.*"

"I loved being a travel agent," Koemi says. "It was my first and only real job." "What happened then?" Ainsley asks.

Koemi looks down and fiddles with her hands. "I... sort of kept sending people to the wrong places by accident."

More laughter ensues—except from Borbola, who sticks her chest out and points at herself. "Borbola has her love waiting for her in Russia. In the cold." Even *I* roll my eyes. We all honestly think Borbola is lying about being in a long-distance relationship. She is always going on about how hurt she was by an ex from years and years ago. We don't think she's capable of being in a relationship. "All I want is to settle down with him. In small home. Sip warm soup.

Stir the fire. Be cozy."

"That's... nice, Borb," Dejuan says, side-eyeing the others.

"What about you?" Borbola asks him.

"Me?" Dejuan shakes his head. "You guys know my family wants me to be a doc just like them."

“Don’t they think that’s what you’re off doing?” I ask. Mr. and Mrs. McGee think he is a traveling physician, something they expect him to do for a living. He takes free online courses here and there to keep up the medical lingo/lie. He’s our team’s medic because of this.

“Yeah.” He shrugs.

“What do you really want to do?” Koemi asks, bright-eyed.

“I dream of being a pro athlete.”

Frankie snorts. “Fuggetabout it! You’re the least athletic guy in the group. And that includes me!” He does a wheelie in his chair.

“You guys don’t know what I’m capable of,” he says, getting defensive. “I’m waiting for my big break. It’ll happen. You all just wait and see.” He goes back to spraying the air with disinfectant, making everyone go into a coughing fit.

Dejuan is also a bit of a germaphobe.

“Get out of ‘ere with zat!” Remy demands.

“I know you of all people would rather the insects stayed away, am I wrong?” Dejuan fires back.

Remy crosses his arms.

I shake my head, waving away the disinfectant mist. “Come on, Dejuan. There’s something I need to discuss with you in my room, anyhow.”

“Take that spray with you!” Frankie calls as we walk away from the group.

CHAPTER 3

Dejuan and I step into my room, away from the rest of the team. He's basically second in command here—the only other person in the group I really trust. The only smart one even when he's fully dressed—unlike myself. My smarts and cunning? It only happens butt naked.

"Guessing you want to talk about our last showdown?" Dejuan asks. "What a disaster it was?"

"The plan was good, but yeah, it was ugly." I nod my head, catching my reflection in the cracked mirror bolted to the wall. My curly hair is long overdue for a cut. I think I've gotten even paler. Have I lost weight? I didn't think I could get much skinnier. Maybe I got taller.

"We need to work better together," he tells me. "We can't keep traveling at this pace.

We'll run out of places to go. If the police ever catch on to us, we'll go to jail."

"I agree. I was actually thinking maybe I should step down as the team leader. Since we failed so badly last time."

"Absolutely not." He shakes his head. "You're a great leader, Jeffery. We all think so."

"Only when I'm naked."

"When it *counts*," he corrects. "But maybe we need to figure out everyone else's roles.

Or, a real team name. Get more organized. I don't know. What do you think?"

"Give everyone roles?" I scratch my chin. God, what roles could these circus clowns have? What could I assign everyone when they're all such a mess? We're *all* such a mess.

Here's the rundown on the team.

Dejuan McGee (Age 24)

Superpower: Turns neon green and swells with fatness and stickiness. Provides armor, sort of.

Although it doesn't stop bullets, it absorbs bullets without causing pain or damage to Dejuan.

Activation: Being startled, attacked, etc.

Weakness/Limitations: Everything—and I mean *everything*—gets stuck to him when he's in his superpower form.

Borbola Egorov (Age 53)

Superpower: Super strength. The closer her bladder is to uncontrollable release, the stronger she becomes.

Activation: Her bladder must be full-bursting. It doesn't activate until she has to urinate. **Weakness/Limitations:** Sort of hard for her to focus when she has to pee so bad. And she goes back to normal after she finally bursts. Ruins a lot of clothes and personal belongings.

Ainsley Tilley (Age 32)

Superpower: Super speed. The drunker he is, the faster he becomes.

Activation: Requires excessive alcohol in his system.

Weakness/Limitations: Well, drunk people aren't the most coherent, stable, or right-minded, now are they?

Koemi Doi (Age 19)

Superpower: Can temporarily utilize attributes of any type of animal/creature.

Activation: Must consume a sample of the animal or its lineage to activate (e.g., eats fish = can swim and breathe underwater).

Weakness/Limitations: She also has IBS and doesn't like many foods. While using her power, she has no control over how long it lasts or what level it can be used at.

Wekesa Afumba (Age 27)

Superpower: Can produce a skunk-like odor from his butt. The stench is so strong it causes blindness, burning of the eyes, uncontrollable vomiting, loss of consciousness, etc.

Activation: Being startled, attacked, etc.

Weakness/Limitations: His butt becomes raw and tender the longer he uses his power.

Remy Rousseau (Age 25)

Superpower: Can talk to and understand insects.

Activation: Automatically active.

Weakness/Limitations: Some insects don't like him and try to force Remy to do things for them. Endless pestering occurs if he doesn't comply. Before he got his power, he was grossed out by crickets. Now, he and crickets have a complicated relationship. Remy hates the sound they make at night—sometimes they do it just to annoy him.

Trish Stanley (Age 38)

Superpower: Can turn into an unbreakable statue and feel nothing.

Activation: Can activate at will but can't control the duration.

Weakness/Limitations: This drains her and leaves her exhausted each time. She often falls asleep on missions and turns into a sleeping statue at inconvenient times.

Frankie Caruso (Age 44)

Superpower: Can fly with his wheelchair while playing a phone game he doesn't even like anymore.

Activation: Has to be playing the game on his phone (think Angry Birds meets Candy Crush).

Weakness/Limitations: Must be actively playing the game for the power to work. Also has a fear of heights, large bodies of water, quicksand, mud, and busy intersections.

Dejuan and I stand there trying to figure out how each team member could do better for future missions, given a specific job. But it's not going well.

Ah ha—I might have a way to fix that.

Thinking fast, I pull my pants down with my boxers.

"C'mon man, we talked about this, you gotta warn me first." Dejuan is caught off guard. I don't know why. It's not like this is a new thing. In fact, I never get embarrassed or shy when I need to undress. It's nothing they haven't all seen before a hundred times.

I finish stripping.

Now, the cogs are turning. The flow of my superhuman thinking pulsing through my brain.

Oh shoot. This happens sometimes. Where I completely shift gears inside my head, thinking of something unrelated to why I got naked in the first place. It has me thinking of ways to help the team, how to obtain my dream job, and ways to use my superintelligence out in public, all simultaneously. It's easy for me to do, but my heart tugs me in different directions. What's best for me? Versus what's best for the team or what's best for the people needing saving.

I hold up a finger, my posture and overall demeanor entirely changed into someone confident and capable. "You know what I think?"

"Here we go," Dejuan mutters.

"I'll work from home. So I can fully harness my cognitive abilities. Interviews will be conducted by phone only. I'll make sure of it."

Dejuan raises an eyebrow. "...But didn't that back fire last time you tried?"

***

"I wouldn't say it's an inferiority complex by any means, I just tend to have better ways of arriving at optimal conclusions is all," I said to my potential new boss as I sat naked in front of the computer. I found the perfect filter to use beforehand that make it appear to him that I was fully clothed—ingenious idea if you ask me. "I can't conceptualize another 'weakness'. I strongly believe that—"

BANG

The bedroom door flew open. My heart leapt right out of my chest as I jumped up and turned around, thinking we were under attack.

"Wekesa farted during a scary movie, now my face is on fire!" Trish cried, her eyes covered with her hands, tears and snot streaming down her face.

"Good God!" my potential future boss cried out behind me.

My stomach plummeted. The filter!

I looked over my shoulder. Sure enough, my bare ass had filled the screen on his end.

***

"That wasn't an optimal outcome, I'll admit," I say to Dejuan, tapping a finger to my chin. "If I have to do a video interview, I'll just angle the camera so it's above my collarbone.

And I'll lock the door."

"So… you want to leave the team, too?" Dejuan asks.

"Wouldn't it be an ideal situation if we could all live our lives in the ways we'd prefer?"

"But what about… saving people?"

He has a point. I do enjoy that bit of my life. When I'm successful in it, anyhow.

I sigh. "This is all on Ainsley," I point out. "He's the one who is always talking about discarding us all like waste needing to be flushed out. And because everyone admires his tenacity and appearance and godhaveyou, they want to agree with him."

"You seem like you're one of them."

I put a hand on his shoulder. "I want to do both." We're always looking for more ways to establish a better stream of income. Moving to a new place means we all need to find our new "Regular day jobs" anyhow. "For now, I doubt anyone is going anywhere. But we should keep an eye out on Ainsley during our job searches. I might need to entrust you to that, seeing as I'll be holed up here majority of the time. He might try and find something that gives him an out of being a part of the team. And if he goes..." Dejuan sags. "Others might follow." I give him a stern nod.

"Uh... Jeff?" he asks after a beat.

"Hmm?"

"Maybe keep your hand off my shoulder when you're naked?"

CHAPTER 4

I'm holed up here at headquarters —naked as usual— trying to find a job where I can be home all the time. It's not exactly ideal for me to not be out with the rest of the team, who have gone off on their own, split into two groups, to scout the new town and search for some simple job opportunities. But this is their chance to really show off and hone what makes them shine.

After all, they won't only be scouting for jobs.

They'll be scouting for crime!

The first group consists of Trish, Frankie, Wekesa, and Borbola. I let Borbola know ahead of time that she's in charge. She's got that whole motherly thing going for her anyway.

She'll be able to keep them in check.

"This city is a little smaller than I'm used to," Trish says, her eyes wide as saucers as she stares at the super Mart sitting before them. She's imagining all the Twinkies and Ho Hos she'll be able to get her hands on once she's inside, all the while pretending like she's someone trying to avoid paparazzi. "But this market is the biggest I've ever seen!" She claps and squeals with delight.

Between the eye center, nail salon, bakery, pharmacy, and grocery department, these four all feel there could be something here simple for them—at least until they find the job they really want. Trish thinks scanning groceries is suitable for a star who hasn't been discovered yet to do. Especially since she'll always be surrounded by snacks. Frankie's interested in the bakery. Don't know that he'll get hired if they make him bake them a tester treat first—Frankie's goodies aren't exactly... edible.

Wekesa wants to work in the perfume department, so he can gather intel for his future perfumery he hopes to one day own. Borbola chose to be a greeter. She has the biggest R.B.F.

face known to mankind though, so not sure how that will pan out either.

"You gotta be kiddin' me," Frankie grumbles, throwing his hands up in the air in irritation when he spots something across the store, over by the electronics.

The others' heads turn to see what he's complaining about this time. A young teen, dressed in all black, with a skateboard and a large black backpack, is stuffing video games and computer accessories into the bag, looking around repeatedly to make sure no one can see him. He has no idea yet that from across the way, he has been spotted. By the Supers—okay, name's still a work in progress.

"Looks like we're gonna have to put job hunting on a little hold," Wekesa says, grinning mischievously and steepling his fingers as he stares the kid down.

The rest of the group—Remy, Koemi, Dejuan, and Ainsley—stroll down a downtown avenue, eyes peeled for opportunities.

"Check this out," Dejuan says, stopping them with a hand. They follow his gaze to an alley, where a mugger's got a woman at knifepoint.

They all exchange a look of understanding.

"*Now*, Jeff isn't *here*," Dejuan reminds them as Ainsley pulls out a flask, Koemi digs out a 'Bowl-O-Noodles', and

Remy calls to nearby insects. “Let’s stick to our strengths. Ainsley, use your speed to grab that lady and bring her back to me. I’ll use my power to shield her. Koemi, eat your beef noodles and ram the mugger like a bull. Remy, have your flies bring the lady’s purse back from the mugger, when Koemi sends him flying.”

Ainsley chugs, while Koemi downs her noodles, uncooked and without water. “Gross.” Koemi complains.

After a few wobbles, Ainsley takes off—immediately crashing into a dumpster. The robber snaps his head back to see Ainsley struggle to stand back up. The two look eye to eye for a moment.

Dejuan turns to Koemi. “Are you—” Koemi stands with fish-like fins and lifts her noodle package to see it was actually shrimp flavored, not beef. “CRAP!” Dejaun yells. Ainsley bursts out like a rocket and grabs the woman then,

SMACK.

He and the lady hit a brick wall and are knocked unconscious.

Koemi’s legs are replaced with the shrimp bottom, as she, slowly, bounces toward Ainsley to help.

Dejuan inflates into a neon green blob, rolling forward and picking up trash, a traffic cone, and someone's gym bag. He's not getting there anytime soon.

Remy throws his arms out. "My loyal subjects! Bring me the purse, now!" The swarm of wasps immediately start buzzing angrily.

"You question me? ...your master? I command you!" Remy shouts, arguing with what looks like the air, before the wasps turn on him and sting him all over.

The mugger, in disbelief, sees a shrimp-human hybrid, a blob, and a man yelling at

wasps—then screams and bolts in the other direction, dropping the woman's purse to the ground.

"Technically," Dejaun huffs, "we stopped him?"

Koemi flops to her side like a fish out of water. Who knows how long it'll last.

"Great," Remy complains. "How are vee going to walk around our new town weeth a large shrimp and a passed out drunk?"

"Dunno, but we gotta get out of here before the lady wakes up and calls the cops." Dejuan says as he slaps Ainsley to wake.

Back in the supermarket, the team decides to block the thief in on one isle, while remaining inconspicuous.

Trish turns into a statue on one end, while Frankie and Borbola close in one him from the other end. Wekesa keeps an eye out from the perfume section.

The teenager, catches on to what's happening and does a kickflip over Trish on his skateboard.

"Freeze!" Borbola cries. "Your mother would be ashamed!" She tries using only her words to make him stop, since he's out of her reach (and she doesn't have to pee yet, so her muscles are useless). "Ugh. I need to hydrate."

"Where's Ainsley when you need him?" Frankie asks, unable to use his flying ability at the moment because it would draw too much attention. He wheels after the kid, yelling at him and calling him a punk. Wekesa snatches up a perfume bottle and tries to blind the kid with its spray as he skates by, but the skater gets so close to him, looking about to run him over, that Wekesa cries out, startled, and a burst of tear gas–like odor tears a hole in his red jeans.

"Dude! That's rank! My eyes are burning!" the kid cries, as he crashes through the front entrance of the store, and setting off the security alarms. The teenager manages to stumble away with the goods, Scott free.

Customers and employees look toward the front entrance to see what's happening. Borbola, Wekesa and Frankie look at one another and nod in agreeance. Frankie bolts out of a back entrance, pulls out his phone, and takes off to the skies back home. Borbola and Wekesa try to lift Trish's statue but she's too heavy. Instead, they decide to use the crowd commotion as a distraction to exit unnoticed.

Later, at closing time, the store employees look baffled at the random statue blocking one of the isles. It's too heavy to move. "I've never seen this statue before. We'll get a forklift to move in the morning." the supervisor says.

CHAPTER 5

It's been three days without much luck. We're all a little stressed, what with needing money to—you know—survive. Sure, we've been doing what we all came together to do in the first place, which is stopping crime. But even that's all been 50/50, and it's always little things, like shoplifters or litterers.

I'm taking a break from my own job search to help some of the gang on their quests. Mainly because I have nothing better to do—our internet is down. While the team is out, I'll sneak away on a quick little trip back home, and be back before anyone knows I was missing.

We've enlisted Frankie to stay back and call the internet provider to get it taken care of.

"Youse guys want me to make my famous muffins?" Frankie asks as we're all throwing on shoes and jackets by the barely-hanging-on front door. We really need to fix that. "You'll want a snack while youse walkin' in town."

There's a lull. We all start looking around at each other, making faces. Frankie's got his back turned to us over in our makeshift kitchen, so he can't see us. Wekesa's mouth opens, but I interrupt before he can.

"Aw, thanks, Frankie! But we've already eaten! Earlier. Uh, before you woke up."

It's a lie, but it's surely better than whatever Wekesa had been about to say. The thing is, Frankie's "famous muffins" might be famous for an entirely different reason than the one he's thinking.

They're terrible.

It's like eating rocks with raisins embedded in them. I think Borbola chipped a tooth on one once.

Frankie shrugs, starting to get out the supplies to make them anyway. "Suit yaselves."

"Why doesn't anyone ever tell him he needs to just give up his baking dream?" Ainsley asks in a whisper, shaking his head. "Poor chap."

Trish crinkles her nose. "He's never made anything good."

"Aw, come on," Koemi squeaks out, her eyes getting big, "yes he has!"

Everyone gapes at her. Wekesa crosses his arms. We wait for her to give an example.

"Um… there was that—no, that was no good. Okay… ooh! What about those—oh, wait.

The sausage loaf wasn't too bad. I only threw up once after eating it."

Wakesa corrects her. "That was his lemon loaf."

"Oh. Um…" She trails off, still looking hopeful as she tries to think of something, but eventually, she hangs her head and shakes it almost imperceptibly.

Remy snorts. "Zat's what I thought."

Meanwhile, Frankie is so busy humming as he clangs pots and pans around that he doesn't hear us.

We leave, giving Frankie the warehouse to himself. He sings Sinatra loudly, gets the muffin batter made, and then throws it into the portable oven plugged into a generator before he makes the call to their internet provider.

"Huh," he says to himself when he hangs up, feeling accomplished for providing help for the team, "If Borbola is like the mother of the team, I'm like their father." He shudders. "Not that I'd ever wanna be Borb's husband. Not gonna go and be with someone who can lift more than I can. No thank youse."

He shakes his head and continues baking while waiting for the technician to arrive at their warehouse.

"Um... hello?" a womanly voice asks through the hanging open door. "Is someone there?

Was this a prank call?"

Frankie wheels around the kitchen, and that's when she comes into his view; a literal angel, the sun shining in behind her, illuminating her. Just like Frankie, the gorgeous brunette is in a wheelchair, a fancy motorized one. She's positively radiant in her cobalt blue collared shirt and khaki pants. Her silver nametag reads "Meg."

"Hiya there," Frankie says, completely awestruck by her. In the kitchen, the muffins begin to burn. Frankie doesn't even notice it. Because the second their eyes met, it was as if they both went into some sort of lovestruck trance.

"Youse... uh... here to... fix... our... internet?" Frankie slowly manages to spit out.

"I am, I'm the owner, actually. I wanted to come see what the problem was for myself.

And I must say, I'm glad I did."

"Boy, so am I."

They continue to stare at each other with no words being said for frankly far too long. Meg finally cuts in, "What kind of issues are you having?" Frankie, still in a trance, speaks monotone, "Just a little rusty, I haven't been on a date in a while, ya know?"

Meg, looking confused, "That's what you need the internet for?"

Frankie finally snaps out of it, "OH! NO! I need it to search for a job. I prefer to bake,

but..."

She takes a deep inhale. The air is a mixture of rotten eggs and muffins about to catch fire. But she seems to drink it up like a love potion.

"I'd love to have you work for me..."

"Name's Frankie," he says, wheeling closer to her, smiling his "sexy smirk" for her.

She blushes. "Or..." she wheels closer to him. "You could just come stay with me and bake me goodies all day."

It's safe to say—Frankie is in love.

"For you, Meg, I'd move mountains."

CHAPTER 6

"I totally got this." Koemi checks her reflection in her small pink compact mirror before dropping it into her purse. She managed to borrow the group's big van and drive herself all the way here, parking safely and correctly in the parking garage of the tall skyscraper where her interview is being held. She takes a second to admire her cute, yet professional, outfit, giggles, and walks toward the elevators.

Koemi misses her job as a travel agent. Sending people off on their dream vacations had always been such a treat—even if she was confused half the time and always making mistakes. This new job she's after isn't anything similar to a travel agent, but she's been feeling the pressure from the rest of the group to get herself employed, so she's settling for whatever she can get.

"Oooh, I hope I get there on time for once," she says as she speed walks, her heels clicking loudly on the pavement. She's had four other interviews that she didn't make or was late to either because she got lost or distracted. Yesterday, she saw a cute dog at a coffee shop as she walked past, so she pet it and then began asking it for a pep talk. "You'd hire me, right, Mr.

Fluffyface?"

Ended up being 23 minutes late. The interviewer wouldn't even see her.

Day before that, she followed another woman dressed like she was going to an interview and so she figured it would be safe to just follow her to where she was going, since they were in another very large skyscraper. She ended up sitting in on a pyramid scheme pitch for over an hour before she suddenly realized she wasn't in the right place whatsoever. By then, she'd missed the interview entirely.

Koemi stops in front of the elevators. There are multiple. And beside them is some sort of machine with a screen and keypad. "Oh." She steps in front of the computer. "Must be where I check in." She waves a hand in front of it, smiling brightly, trying to look prepared and ready.

"My name is Koemi Doi! I am here for my interview?"

Someone taps her on the shoulder. She turns to find an old man. "Miss, that's where you pay for parking."

Koemi's face heats up. She smiles through her embarrassment. "Oh! Thank you!"

They ride the elevator up together. He wishes her luck on his stop. She gets off somewhere close to the top and for once, makes it to the interview in time.

It goes well. So well, in fact, that when Koemi mentions she has IBS when it's in no way relevant to the current discussion, the interviewer, Micah, doesn't bat an eye. "You have IBS? I have Crohn's!" They laugh about it.

"Tell you what," Micah says toward the end, shifting in his high-backed fancy rolling desk chair, a brilliant view of the city behind him just outside his floor-to-ceiling windows of his office. "You seem like you really loved your position as a travel agent."

"Oh, I most definitely did!"

He smiles. "Instead of this boring desk job you're interviewing for, I actually have a travel agent position that would be perfect for you!"

Koemi frowns, feeling slightly disheartened. “But, Mr. Jones—”

“Please, call me Micah.”

She giggles. “But Micah, sir, I was fired for sending people to the wrong destinations.

Multiple times.”

He waves a dismissive hand. “This position is even more perfect for you then. I have some rich clients who are looking to be surprised.”

“Wh... whaaaa?”

“That’s right! It doesn’t matter where you send them! How does that sound?” Koemi couldn’t believe it. It sounded too good to be true.

CHAPTER 7

Dejuan balls his fists as he walks alongside Ainsley into the commercial building that houses the temp agency. "You know, I think you and Remy are being incredibly selfish," he says, unable to help himself. He's tried to hold it in, but it has to come out.

"Oh, *do* go on," Ainsley replies, not even glancing up from his phone. "What's life without a guilt trip or two from your unofficial babysitter? I know you've been requested by

Jeffery to follow me around."

Dejuan doesn't bother denying it. "I'm serious. You know how much of an influence you have on the rest of the team. You're making them want to call it quits, too.

We're supposed to stick together, Ainsley. Solve crime and work normal jobs. That's what superheroes do."

Ainsley smirks, adjusting the collar of his bomber jacket. "I don't do normal, D. And being in that dump of a place with the lot of you? That's worse than normal. Let's face it: being a 'team' hasn't really been working out for us, has it? What's our win count? Five out of a hundred or something?"

Dejuan shakes his head. "Man, you're exaggerating."

They enter the lobby, and it's not exactly a very inspiring place. It's like everything's been washed in gray. *Great*, Dejuan thinks to himself, seeing the way Ainsley shakes his head disapprovingly as he grits his teeth. *This kind of place is* not *Ainsley's scene.*

Dejuan scribbles his name on the sign-in sheet while Ainsley leans against the counter, acting too cool to be in a place so "below" him. It makes Dejuan scoff. Ainsley thinks he's hot stuff. But he's no better than the rest of the team.

A woman in a headset waves them over. "Mr. Tilley, you're next."

Ainsley fixes his hair in the reflection of the vending machine, gives the woman a seductive wink, and strolls through the interview room door. The woman swoons.

Dejuan takes a seat and sighs. Maybe he's a little bitter because he's never had that effect on women. Hell, even the man with slicked-back hair standing next to the receptionist can't seem to take his eyes off him.

The sharply dressed, good-haired man disappears, and then he comes back ten minutes later, passing Dejuan as he strolls right up to the room Ainsley's being interviewed inside. He pushes it open and leans into the room. "Mr. Tilley? Would you step outside with me a moment?"

Ainsley comes out into the hallway. Dejuan gets to his feet, suspicious.

"You're wasting your time in there," the man says. "You don't strike me as someone meant to shred papers and input data into computers all day."

"Finally, someone who gets me," Ainsley says, clearly intrigued.

"You've got this presence about you. Confidence. You're just the right amount of edgy. Ever thought about—" he lowers his voice so Dejuan has to stick an ear out to hear— "escort work?"

Ainsley raises an eyebrow. "Escort?"

"Private clients. You'll get access to all sorts of events and exclusive parties. You get paid to show up and look good. Surrounded by gorgeous women all the time—

which I am sure you're already used to—but with no strings attached."

Ainsley's grin widens. "Rather sounds like a dream come true, doesn't it?"

"I thought it might." The man hands him a card. "Clients tip well. And I've got a friend— he scouts for modeling gigs. Been looking for someone with your look."

Ainsley turns the card over in his hand, eyes sparkling. "Well, screw the team then."

"You serious right now?" Dejuan's voice cuts in as he marches up. "You'd really leave all of us just like that?"

Ainsley doesn't respond.

The man steps smoothly between them. "Easy. No need for drama, gentlemen." He eyes

Dejuan. "I actually have an opportunity for you, too."

"Man, I've been dealing with his crap all morning. Don't think I've got room for yours too."

The man smiles, undeterred. "You've got strength. Discipline. A calm presence. Sometimes our clients don't like to pay up. I could use someone like you to ensure everything ends... smoothly."

Dejuan blinks. "What, you want me to rough people up for you? Like some sort of bodyguard? For this guy?" Dejuan can't think of anything he'd like less.

"Escort security," the man says casually. "Also, fun fact: my best friend's a producer. He's filming a movie downtown. They need a stuntman. Someone athletic. You ever take a fall down some stairs?"

"Uh… not professionally." Crap. Dejuan can't help it. He's beginning to feel intrigued.

Ainsley nudges him hard with his elbow. "You've always wanted to be an athlete, yeah?"

He wiggles his eyebrows at his babysitter. "Here's your shot."

Dejuan takes the card from Ainsley, eyeing the fancy logo. Babysit Ainsley, shake down clients for a little while, for the chance he'll get to be a real stuntman? He pictured the pay he'd receive and got goosebumps. Finally, a way to prove he's got what it takes. Not just tech nerd babysitter or second-in-command to Jeff, or a fake travel physician like his parents think he is.

And it would be great for Dejuan. If Dejuan didn't need to lie down for fifteen minutes after jogging up one flight of stairs. And he turns into the green blob whenever he's startled.

Being a stuntman, it's easy to imagine he'll be startled a lot.

Dejuan glances at Ainsley, who's looking a lot like his mind is made up.

"Think it over and give me a call." The man disappears around the corner.

Dejuan gives Ainsley back the card. The smug douche slides it into his jacket. "Not bad, right? A little attention, a lot of money, zero weird missions involving bugs or Animal-Girl?" "It does seem... cool," Dejuan can't help but admit.

Ainsley slaps him on the back. "Leaving the team's not sounding so terrible now, is it?"

Dejuan doesn't answer right away. But yeah. He's tempted. Really tempted. But he doesn't want to give Ainsley the satisfaction of knowing that.

"You know what?" he says instead, rolling his eyes at Ainsley as he heads for the exit.

"Now I know why they call it a temp agency. Because I'm *temp*-ted to knock you out."

CHAPTER 8

Wekesa does a very good job minding his own business as he brushes the inner walls of a massive pool at an insanely large, opulent mansion. He's working a temp job as a pool cleaner for the day. Testing it out. Anything for some extra cash—for himself, mostly. Sure, the headquarters needs things—*badly*—but Wekesa has had his eye on this paisley ascot he found online. It's already in the cart. All he has to do is press *purchase*. He doesn't have to tell the group.

What he'd *like* to do while cleaning this pool is fantasize about the ascot, about how good it'll look around his beautiful, slender neck. How people will stare. Wishing they were him—or the ascot.

But it's hard to stay focused when the ultra-wealthy, ultra-*old* woman is lounging poolside in a red two-piece bikini, sunglasses perched low on her nose so she can peer over them at him, a weird smirk on her cherry-red lips.

Wekesa avoids her gaze, swallowing hard as he keeps brushing.

"Oh yeah, I like the way you scrape that," she calls out, wriggling in her chair like she just can't contain herself. Is she... is she trying to *show off* her legs? Her wrinkly, age-spotted legs?!

Wekesa visibly shudders and gives her a stiff smile. Truth is, he has no idea how to clean a pool. He got maybe three minutes of training. His plan: brush the walls, net out the leaves, and call it good.

"I'm sorry you caught me out here during tanning time," she says. So is Wekesa. "But if I don't get my sun every day, I'll be pasty and unwantable." She winks.

He scratches his forehead, trying to decide how to respond. He glances at her again, thinking she was *probably* pretty in her prime. *But hunny*, he thinks, *that was years and years ago. Before I was even born.*

Suddenly, she stands. Wekesa is genuinely surprised she doesn't need a cane.

"You look parched, sweet stuff. Why don't you come inside and let Mama make you lemonade?"

"Mama?" Wekesa arches a brow. "No offense, hunny, but I *absolutely* do not trust going inside with you. Pretty sure you're gonna try to climb me like a tree."

He doesn't expect her to burst into tears. She drops dramatically into her chaise and

weeps into her hands.

"Oh for the love—" Wekesa drops the brush. It slides into the pool, sinking to the deep end. "Fine. Let's go inside."

She clings to his arm as he walks her in, still weeping. He keeps glancing sideways, trying to figure out if she's faking. But she's pushed up her glasses, so it's hard to tell.

Inside, he seats her at a massive white marble table with ornate, gold-lined chairs. He looks around, impressed. This is the kind of place he and the team *should* be staying in between fighting crime. Not some stinky warehouse. This is more his vibe.

"Okay," he says, "you all right? Missed your daily dose of Valium or something?

Husband dead or something?"

He doesn't actually know if she even has a husband.

She removes her glasses.

Wekesa juts his head back. "Ex*cuse me*, ma'am," he says with attitude, "you don't have a *single* tear in those eyes."

She flashes a wicked smile. "Got you in here, didn't I?"

"You're *really* something," he says, mildly impressed. Then he catches a scent. His nostrils flare. It's divine. He slowly turns, taking in perfume bottles, trophies, marketing ads lining the walls.

His mouth drops open.

"You own a perfumery?"

She flips her short, puffy white hair over her shoulder, even though it doesn't even reach it. The move is entirely pointless. "The name's Veronica," she says, offering a dainty hand.

He eyes it with full-body hesitation. *Yeah, no,* he thinks. *Ain't no way my lips are getting anywhere near that.* He gives it a half-hearted shake instead.

"Musky Mischief has been in business for years. I'm a very successful woman, if you can't tell, *darling*."

"That's literally my dream," Wekesa says, placing a hand on his chest, practically glowing with envy. "I'd give *anything* to own my own perfumery."

She scans him from head to toe. Normally, he'd shut that down—*paws off, eyes off*—but right now, she can ogle all she wants.

"Is that so?" she says.

They smile at each other.

"Once my husband, Charles, is out of the picture," she says, her voice low and husky as she rises from the chair and slowly approaches him, all predatory grace, "the perfumery is yours.

He's on life support now. Thinking I'll pull the plug tomorrow."

Wekesa blinks. "Are you playing with me right now?"

She growls softly. "Oh, I'd *love* to play with you."

"I meant the perfumery."

She sighs dramatically. "I mean it, sweet young thing. All yours."

His eyes bug out. He stares, speechless. "You got a deal," he says. And they shake on it.

CHAPTER 9

Remy thinks any good, decent restaurant should be *supremely* clean—free of insects so they don't get in trouble with the health inspector. A place where the insects stay outside, in the alleyway, within reach at a moment's notice if Remy *should* need them, but far enough away so they don't interfere with his ability to get work done. So, becoming a bartender at the local bar seems like a good fit. It's not exactly thrilling, but it's better than bugs. And he needs a job before the team gets mad and says he isn't "pulling his weight."

He's told by the host to sit at the bar and wait for the manager. He puffs out his chest and struts over, trying to look mean, brave, and absolutely not like someone who dines alone and cries into their fries. It's important everyone sees him as a tough guy. Just because he's a *ginger* doesn't mean he's weak. Or sensitive. Or haunted by the fact that sunlight makes him look like a steamed lobster.

And just because he's terrible at stopping crime doesn't mean it's his fault.

It's the *team's* fault. Obviously.

A chirp sounds in his ear. *"Think you can snag me a bite to eat?"* Remy turns and sees a cockroach perched on his shoulder.

"What ze—!" He flicks the thing off. "*What* kind of establishment is zis?" His face is tight with disgust as he waits for the manager. The manager he fully intends to scold for having *a roach problem*.

He glances over his shoulder. A group of men in boating attire sit glumly around a table. He watches as one of them, clearly defeated, gets up and walks to the bar, waiting for the pretty blonde bartender to finish with the others.

Remy forgets all about the cockroach. He raises an eyebrow. "Where did you all come from? And I know I'm not ze bartender, but—eh, why ze long faces?"

The guy slumps onto the stool next to him, uninvited. The big, burly sailor rests an elbow gloomily on the bar and sinks his chin into it. “We just got back to shore.” “You were on a boat?” Remy is instantly intrigued.

The guy nods. “And we had a brilliant captain. Emphasis on *had*.”

“What 'appened to 'im?” Remy doesn’t actually care. He’s more excited by the idea that they’re in need of a captain.

“He was eaten. By a mysterious monster at sea.”

“You are *kidding*.” Remy clears his throat, sits up taller. “You know, I 'appen to 'ave excellent sailing skills. I was captain of my own ship once. Lost my crew.”

“Oh yeah?” the man asks. “What happened to *them*?”

***

Remy and Trish stands across from a car thief limping out of a wrecked stolen car. Remy scans the rest of his team with a look of disgust on his face.

Koemi lies on the ground, temporarily paralyzed from eating a veggie pizza and using her power, “Sorry guys”.

Dejaun slowly rolls around the ground like a giant nose booger, that accumulated too much trash to effectively control his motor functions. "I can't move! Somebody help!"

Frankie, a couple hundred yards back, is trying to reattach a wheel onto his wheelchair from it being knocked off by the car thief hitting him with the stolen car. "I'm coming! Just hold on youse guys!"

"Get him!" Trish yells out before her and Remy charge towards the thief. After a few quick slaps by the thief, Trish is stunned and calls out to Remy, "I'm going to fall on him and hold him down with my power." The thief and Remy look at one another in understanding.

"Trish! Don't! He knows what—"

It's too late, Trish leans towards the thief and turns into a statue. The thief easily steps aside letting her fall face flat to the ground.

The thief slams Remy against the stolen car and beats him unconscious, while nearby crickets watch and laugh.

The thief takes off running and gets away.

Koemi innocently mutters from the ground "Guys? ...what happened? ...did we catch him?"

***

Remy glares in contempt. "...Zey are dead to me."

The man heaves a deep sigh. "It's a shame. We've got this beautiful boat, all the resources we need, but no one to lead us to the X."

"Ze X?"

"On our map. We need a captain. We're useless without one. Good old Captain

Woodteeth... He had been about to lead us on a famously dangerous treasure hunt. Oh, the riches we're missing out on..."

Remy forgets all about the bartending gig. Forgets why he even came here. He leaps up from his stool and pounds his chest. "You 'ave found yourself a *new* captain!"

The man grins and turns to his crewmates. "You guys hear that?"

They erupt in a hearty cheer. The man next to Remy—who introduces himself as Chip— buys a round of pints. Remy joins them at their table. They clink glasses and break into a sea shanty. Remy feels right at home.

He can't believe it. He's finally going to get his hands on treasure. *Real* treasure.

The crew explains the boat needs some repairs, but they plan to leave tonight. They tell Remy where to meet them.

Remy thinks it's the best news he's heard in ages. Nothing but the open ocean. Any insects that bother him aboard? He'll make them *walk ze plank*.

He won't have to deal with those pain-in-the-asses anymore.

CHAPTER 10

I sit at a table alone in a coffee shop, filling out a job application to be a "barista." Or *trying* to, anyway. I'm mostly just sweating. A lot. I'm on question two, which is "Phone Number," and I've erased it three times because I keep second-guessing my own area code.

This would be so much easier if I was naked.

Then again, I'd probably get the cops called on me.

Again.

Can't a guy just be naked in public if it's for the greater good?

I know, I know—a barista job isn't a work-from-home situation. But I haven't found anything yet. And I don't have a whole lot of time to keep searching. My thoughts about a job at a place like this are—how hard can it be? All

I gotta do is pour coffee in a cup. Right? I can keep my clothes on for that.

I think the guy behind the counter can tell I'm a fraud. He keeps glancing at me with this look like he knows I am not in any way qualified for this position.

Sigh. He's probably right. In clothes, I'm not cut out to do much of anything. The customer service industry would eat me alive. What if someone asks for an "iced" coffee? Then what am I supposed to do? I can't handle that!

I pretend to sip my coffee, which is awful because I actually hate coffee in any form, and open my phone to distract myself with emails. It's mostly junk.

Wait.

My heart skips a beat.

Subject: Conditional Acceptance – Ridge Valley Community College

You've gotta be kidding me. This can't actually be *real*, can it?

I open it, read the first two lines, then reread them because I got too excited to pay attention. But I *got in*. I actually *got in*. Ridge Valley Community College has accepted me.

Conditionally, sure, but who cares?

When I went out with the gang on their job searches back when Frankie waited for the internet lady, I snuck off and hitched a cab to my hometown. I figured the reason I haven't been selected for any of these work-from-home jobs I've been applying to is because I don't have a college degree. I had to test in person for the community college. And somehow, without being naked, I passed the admissions test!

"HAH!" I honk out, immediately looking around, embarrassed about the outburst. People are definitely staring at me. Whoops. The barista raises one eyebrow. I raise my cup and nod like I am perfectly capable of playing it cool, but then I immediately burn my tongue when I slurp down too much coffee at once, and it spills out of my mouth and down my shirt. Huh. I guess for once it's a good thing I'm fully clothed.

My excitement dies down a little when I think about the team. Because the thing is... I love the team. I love fighting crime. I love the stupid way we all yell over each other during planning and never agree until I take charge—nude. I love being their leader—even though my plans usually never pan out.

But we're all… drifting. I can feel it. Ainsley thinks he's too hot for us. Borbola keeps droning on in third person about missing her "love"—whoever that is—and Dejuan's dying to prove to his parents he can make it in this world without being the traveling physician they think and expect him to be. I'm afraid none of them really want to keep doing this anymore. It's lonely. It sucks. It's like I'm still playing with the G.I. Joe dolls when everyone else outgrew them and moved on to… I don't know, *bigger* G.I. Joe dolls.

Maybe if I leave first, it won't hurt so bad. If I'm the one to say goodbye, I won't be the one left behind.

I sniff, feeling the waterworks coming on. I go to wipe my eyes and knock the entire mug off the table. It shatters on the hardwood. Coffee flies everywhere. Behind the counter, the barista sighs audibly. I mouth "sorry" and try to bend down in my chair and clean it with a napkin.

I fall out of the chair and land on the glass shards and in the hot puddle.

Time for me to just get the heck out of here.

I don't think I was cut out for this job anyway.

I walk out into the sunlight with my heart pounding and my mind racing. I'm gonna do this. When I get back to headquarters, I am going to make my announcement.

It's time for me to leave. College—*community* college—here I come.

CHAPTER 11

Trish is *supposed* to be job hunting.

That's what she told the team. She told everyone she needs a few hours to herself to "get serious" about securing a day job like the others have been doing. Of course, she said this while chowing down on Twinkies on the sofa, globs of white filling stuck to the hot pink tracksuit—its jacket zipper and pants drawstring hanging on for dear life around her wide frame.

She opens her laptop. She has the best intentions. Truly. But somehow, she finds herself accidentally opening her bookmarked folder titled IFLUENCERS FOR INSPO. Before she knows it, she's got a dozen open tabs of influencer profiles and Mukbang TikToks, and not a single job application or search for open positions.

Also on one of her tabs is her social media page. She refreshes it. Once. Then again, hoping to find that *finally*, her cousin Todd isn't her only follower. She really could do without his deeply inappropriate comments under every post.

She decides to type up a new status: *Big news coming soon... stay tuned ;) #BookedAndBusy #HollywoodHereICome.*

So what if she's full of it? People lie on social media all the time, right? Besides, she's trying to *manifest* here, people.

Then her phone dings.

She gasps and immediately clutches her chest, her heart hammering, making her think maybe she shouldn't have had those six Twinkies. Or those two salted pretzels at the mall. Or the Slurpee on the way to the mall. Or the microwave corndog she heated up before she left to get the Slurpee on her way to the mall.

She has a new direct message. It's from an account that definitely looks legit—to Trish. The handle is @HOLLYWOODREALCASTING_NOW606. The profile pic is the star-eyes emoji.

She opens it.

HELLO BEAUTIFUL WOMAN!!!

We saw ur profile and were BLOWN AWAY!!!

You have STAR ENERGY!!! Are you ready to be FAMOUS??

Casting for HOT NEW SHOW: **HOUSE OF BEAUTIFULS**

Seeking VIBRANT females 18–50 (flexible) for reality TV magic

Filming TONIGHT — exclusive, secret location. No one can know your whereabouts

(turn that location off on ur phone, lol!)

Transportation provided. Meet at pickup point near you

Must have charisma, bold spirit, strong feet, and open mind

NO EXPERIENCE NEEDED

Free snacks on site and chance to meet CELEBRITY guest

DM ASAP to change your LIFE

– Brandon (Real Person), Celebrity Scout

Sure, it's a questionable message to anyone with half a brain and not desperate for fame.

To Trish, this message is a dream come true. *Finally.*

She squeals lightly, doing a little dance in her seat—okay, more like a small jostle that gets her out of breath, so she stops just as quickly as she started. She reads the message again. She has *zero* questions about the offer. Absolutely *no* warning bells going off in her head. She's not the *slightest* bit suspicious. Trish doesn't even feel the need to Google the show or check the messenger's profile.

She types back that she's in. They tell her where to go for pick-up and when to get there. She wishes it didn't have to be so late in the night before she starts on her destiny, but she isn't about to complain.

She heads to her curtained-off bedroom in the warehouse and pulls out a leopard print suitcase. *Time to start packing.*

She throws articles of clothing and shoes onto her bed. Sequin dresses, cat-eye sunglasses. Feather boas. She even grabs some rock-hard brownies Frankie baked and throws them into a Ziploc bag. *It's better to arrive with a present for the producer*, she thinks.

She turns and catches herself in her full-length double-wide mirror. “This is it,” she tells her reflection. “My moment. My close-up.”

She cannot *wait* for tonight. Wherever “tonight” is. Whatever “transportation provided” means. She plans to be early and in full glam—but let’s be real, when is she not?

She’s too excited to even be sad about leaving the team behind. Finally, Trish is getting her big break.

CHAPTER 12

I'm ready for this. I'm totally ready for this.

Okay, I'm *so* not ready for this.

I clear my throat in front of the team. We all stand around the living area of headquarters. Everyone's eyes are on me. I can't help but notice that the others seem exceptionally squirmy or uninterested—or dazed and confused.

"Thank you all for taking the time to meet with me tonight," I start off by saying, feeling how damp my shirt is under my armpits from nerves. *See*? It's good that I'm leaving. I can't even handle talking to this group of people I've known forever!

"I mean... we sort of live here," Frankie says. "We were gonna be here anyway."

I point a finger at him. "Thank you for that, Frankie..." I tug at the collar of my shirt and clear my throat again. "Anyway. You see... I have some news to share."

"Funny, as do I," Remy says, sticking his nose up in the air, looking rather pompous.

To my surprise, everyone around the room starts mumbling and commenting on how they have something to say as well. I feel a little bit relieved about it, because I'm not sure I was ready to tell them all my news yet. It'll be better for them to get whatever they need off their chest first. Maybe it'll make it easier for me to tell them what I have to.

"Okay, all right, s–settle down," I stutter. It takes a little while for them to actually quiet down and listen to me again. "One by one, why don't you all say whatever it is you want before I go?"

Wekesa steps into the circle first, doing a hair flip with both sides of his head, even though his hair is actually very close-shaven. "I just wanted to say that I've always wanted to open up a perfumery, as you all know. And the opportunity fell into my lap. Without any regrets—I mean, without any *hard feelings*—I will be leaving the team."

Nobody looks surprised or astonished. I wonder why that is. *I* certainly am sad to hear it.

I didn't even know with certainty that Wekesa was one of the ones wanting out.

"You... you're leaving?" I ask with wide eyes.

He snaps his fingers in a Z formation. "You know it, hunny."

I frown. "Oh—okay... Who's next?"

"I'm leaving too!" Trish blurts out, slapping a hand over her mouth after like she can't believe her outburst. She giggles. "I'm going to be a star. I told you all I was!"

I don't miss the way Frankie, Remy, and Ainsley stifle laughs as they look at each other. Borbola looks utterly confused. Koemi has definitely zoned out. I hardly doubt she even knows what's happening right now.

"I'm leaving to be captain of a new crew," Remy announces. "One zat's actually *capable.*

Unlike zis pathetic mess."

Okay, ouch. I try not to act offended. But I've been trying my best here!

Suddenly, everyone has an out. Borbola is going back to Russia. Koemi gets to be a travel agent again. Ainsley's gonna be a hooker, and Dejuan is apparently gonna be his bodyguard. Frankie is off to bake goodies for the love of his life that he met just recently and probably doesn't even know the last name of. All of them... every single one of them... are going to leave the team.

And just like I was afraid of, I'm the last one standing.

"It's funny," I say, a lump in my throat. I turn my head to disguise the tears in my eyes.

"That was my news, too. I just let you guys break the news first. But I'm also leaving."

There's a beat of silence. Then Ainsley lets out a dramatic sigh and tosses himself onto the couch like he's been waiting years for this. "Well, thank God," he says. "I can't wait to stop bein' some demented Power Ranger with you useless lot."

"Useless?" Trish hisses, sitting on the sofa, too. "*I* was the only one who really *brought* something to this group. No offense, but most of you have *zero* charisma. A superhero team's foundation is *built* on charisma."

"This team's foundation is as weak as that couch you're about to break," Frankie says, snorting. "Actually, I guess that would make it a strong foundation, for how hard it's hangin' on under the weight of you."

"Be nice to Trish," Borbola says to Frankie. "At least *she* can actually bake."

"Ey—yous watch ya mouth about my bakin'. Never heard yous complainin' before. I'll have you know, Meg loves my goodies." Everyone laughs at him.

Koemi raises her hand with a big smile. "I once turned into a koala and got stuck in a tree for nine hours."

We all take a moment and gape at her.

"Um… you all left me there?" she squeaks out, her cheeks turning pink.

"We t'ought you were a raccoon!" Remy yells.

"Who fed her koala meat?" Borbola asks.

"This is why the team's breaking up," I mutter to myself.

"No," Dejuan says, having heard me. "The team's breakin' up 'cause nobody listens when I say we need structure. Or training. Or a mission plan. Y'all just do whatever and then blame somebody else when it all goes sideways."

"Well, how can anything go bloody *right* when *you* turn into a big lime green jelly bean the moment someone speaks a little too loud?" Ainsley says.

"AT LEAST I ABSORB BULLETS FOR ALL OF YOU!" Dejuan screams.

Remy claps his hands. "I love zis. I genuinely do. We should've disbanded ages ago. We are terrible."

Everyone starts nodding.

Great. For once, there's something we all seem to agree on.

CHAPTER 13

"Great," I tell everyone, nodding my head rapidly after we've all seemed to finish up cutting each other down—at least for a few minutes. "Well then. I think… I think, if we're all leaving—tonight or early tomorrow?" I eye each individual teammate—soon-to-be exteammate—and they all nod. "Then I want to propose, uh, maybe… a farewell dinner?" I worry they're not going to like the idea. But I don't want this to be it. It can't be! We have to have an official "goodbye!"

They all look around at each other. Remy's upper lip is curled up in disgust. But that could be because the crickets have started egging him on again—I think I hear some chirping. Dejuan looks away from the group and down at his feet, pushing up his glasses. Koemi smiles blankly. I don't think she heard my question. Frankie's shaking his head and muttering to himself. Wekesa is examining his nails and tapping an impatient foot. Trish is talking to an invisible TV camera off to the side. "I'm *telling* you. Things have been *so* crazy in this house.

Living with other superheroes? *Not* easy."

I guess she's practicing. Who knows.

Borbola is watching Trish with a look of disdain. Ainsley's got a smile on his face. One of excitement. He can't *wait* to be out of here.

Am I the only one who is actually sad? Our crew has been together for a while now.

We all know each other inside and out. We're all *too* comfortable with each other, even.

"I suppose I can get through one last evening together," Trish says, turning back from the "camera." But the way she looks off at no one and eye-rolls tells me she's still pretending she's being filmed.

Everyone else mutters or mumbles their agreements. So we break apart to get ready for our final super team dinner.

I make reservations somewhere nice while standing naked in my bedroom. It makes me smart enough to smooth-talk my way into a nice table last minute. "If possible, a table by the window—studies show ambient natural light enhances serotonin production and menu satisfaction by eighteen percent. Oh, and if your chef has a tasting menu, I'd love to optimize for flavor sequencing. Thank you kindly!"

Over in Borbola's curtained-off room, she taps her chin repeatedly. "Nice outfit for

Borbola tonight. Hmmm..." She has a hard time finding something free of piss stains. Her best bet is another spring dress.

Wekesa chooses something over the top as usual. An ombré rainbow silk polo shirt, turquoise slacks cut to his mid-calf, nails painted bright white, a little glitter in his body lotion. He looks at himself in the mirror and blows himself a kiss before drenching his body in twelve different perfumes.

Frankie puts on jeans and a T-shirt, like he does every day. Because "Frankie doesn't get dressed up for no one ever."

Ainsley has no doubt he'll draw the attention of a pretty waitress at the restaurant, so he spends nearly an hour styling every strand of hair on his head. I think he looks like he got electrocuted. He thinks it's the new 'do all the ladies are loving.

Trish is ridiculous as always. Huge faux fur coat. Sunglasses covering most of her face. Acting like she's worried the paparazzi will be tailing her.

Dejuan's got on slacks and a button-down. But Ainsley complains he doesn't look enough like his bodyguard and makes him put on sunglasses and an earpiece that doesn't work.

Remy dresses like a Navy SEAL from the '50s. Seriously, where did he find that outfit in such a short period of time?

Lastly, Koemi—sweet Koemi—comes out in a bikini. "I thought you said we were having one final splash!" she cries when I tell her she won't be allowed in the restaurant like that. Then she scurries back behind her curtains.

Before we head out, I look around at all of us, me in a suit because why not? Where else am I going to get to wear it? Not to any superhero recognition ceremonies. Not that we'd ever been invited to one before...

Man. We *really* make no sense together.

But at the same time, I also think we couldn't look more like family. Hard to believe

it'll all be over soon.

CHAPTER 14

"Why'd you make the reservation for nine people?" Ainsley asks when we enter #1 Italian Restaurant. I'll admit—it looked a *lot* nicer in the photos. This place looks like it used to be a Village Inn, just with red and white checkered tablecloths thrown over all the tables. Smells of cigarette smoke and... old people. They just have a smell, don't they.

"What do you mean?" I ask the Brit, trying not to sound exasperated. The whole way over, everyone continues to tear into each other. I keep trying to tell myself that's just what we do. That it's out of love.

He nudges Remy in the side and breaks into a grin. "Trish needs two chairs for her fat arse!"

"I do not!" Trish scowls, her face turning pink. She goes to sit in a chair in the waiting

area—

It breaks.

Dejuan, Koemi, Borbola, and I rush over to help her to her feet. The restaurant manager glares at us from over by the kitchen door. The host takes us to our table. Trish grabs an extra chair from a nearby table so she can have one for each cheek.

Ainsley sees this and looks rather pleased with himself as he sits down with the rest of us.

Trish shoots him a glare that he ignores. "Koemi," she says, "did you turn into a raccoon again?!"

Koemi looks down at herself as though double-checking. "I don't think so, why?"

Trish sneers at Ainsley. "Because Ainsley's hair looks like one got into it!" The table laughs.

"Good one," Koemi says, snorting a little, in a really cute way. Only Koemi could snort and it be cute. "Sorry, Ainsley, you sort of deserved that one."

"At least *I* can order a steak without mooing after a bite," Ainsley barks at her. She frowns, deeply offended. But the rest of the table laughs.

"Aw, come on, take a joke, love," he says to her after.

But the roasting keeps going. One insult after another gets hurled around the table, and we all fake-laugh with each other, all smiles to anyone watching us, but all of us simmering under our skin. When Remy teases me about "zat leetle zing" of mine I'm always flashing to the group like some creep, and people agree with him, I feel a little readier to never speak to any of them again.

But I try and ease the tension. Because that's what a good leader should do.

"I can't believe this is the last time we'll hang out as a team." Everyone quiets down and listens to me.

"We've saved a lot of people and stopped a lot of crimes."

Naturally, someone has to cut in and ruin my attempt to make the evening more enjoyable, as usual. This time, it's Wekesa. "Um, sweetie? We've caused *monumental* amounts of damage in the process. Yeah—pretty sure *nobody* likes us."

"Pretty sure?" Frankie asks, talking loudly because that's just how he is. "Hah. I knows for a fact. They never thanked us for saving them, jus' complained about the stuff we damaged."

"Borbola tinks..." Borbola seems like she had been just about to add something to the conversation that would probably only make me feel worse, but her eyes have drifted from the table, along with her ability to finish a thought, apparently.

Remy joins in with something snarky. The group continues arguing.

But the reason Borbola trailed off is because a well-dressed, short, bald, overweight man has just caught her eye. To Borbola, he is the handsomest man she's ever seen. He makes it easy to forget about the man waiting to be reunited with her in Russia—he doesn't actually know she exists anyway.

He beckons her over to the server station, turning and shooing his employee away. Borbola says nothing to the group, and no one really pays her any attention as she makes her way over to the man, almost like an invisible force pulling her toward him, like there is nothing she could do to stop it from happening if she tried. She is magnetized to him somehow.

"You look like you could use some warm soup and a cozy fire," he tells her when she approaches. He's got a thick Italian accent. He's covered in body hair. It peeks out of every article of clothing he has on. His hands are covered in gold rings. Many of his teeth are gold. His nose is large and bulbous. He's perfect. "My name is Vito. Why you waste-a time with men like those, huh? When you could be home wit' me? Gettin' taken care of?"

Borbola feels the sparks flying. The butterflies erupting. She's about to tell him how absolutely perfect that sounds, a huge grin splitting her face. Seeing Borbola smile never happens. Seriously. It looks so wrong.

But then sadness washes over her. "I cannot."

"I don't understand," he tells her, stepping closer. She wants to melt into his arms.

"I am leaving. Back to Russia."

"Why?"

She side-eyes the table. "Due to, eh... vork."

"Stay," he says. "I got-a better job for you."

"And what is dat?"

He eyes the mole on her chin and licks his lips. "You be part-time owner. Wit' me."

"I... I should not. But... oh, I haff never vanted anything more," she says, her voice low and dreamy.

Floored by the generosity, Borbola accepts.

CHAPTER 15

"What in the...?" Dejuan trails off as Borbola returns to the table, looking at her like she's just grown a third eyeball. Everyone's put off because she's smiling. It makes her hardly recognizable.

"Borbola has just met vonderful man," she says, in a daze. "She—"

"EVERYONE FREEZE!"

We all snap our heads toward the door.

No freaking way.

Multiple men with black beanies pulled down over their faces with eyeholes cut out hold guns and aim them around the restaurant. People gasp in fright. Dinnerware clinks and clatters to the tabletops. People cower in their seats, trying to hide under their tables.

But me and my team? We aren't afraid.

"Everyone get up!" one of the men demands. He locks the door to the restaurant and aims the gun wildly in all different directions, like he wishes he could aim it at everyone at once.

"NOW."

We all do as he says. He and his men move us through a door to the back. We go down a long carpeted hallway, then round a corner to a massive bulletproof reinforced steel vault door.

"Open it up!" one of the robbers demands to the owner, who—what the hell? Why's he holding Borbola's hand?!—cautiously makes his way to the door with Borbola and unlocks it.

"Don't want any trouble, gentlemen," he says in his thick Italian accent.

Oh god. He's a mobster, isn't he? I don't mean to stereotype, but *look* at him! Look at his *vault*!

"Everyone in!" one of the bad guys demands. The vault is the same square footage as the restaurant, basically. Instead of tables, booths, and chairs, there are shelves and tables full of money, diamonds, and other highly valuable items. No windows. No other doors out.

Is that a real *Picasso* I see?

I shake my head. What are the chances *this* is where we'd end up having dinner?

"I do not understand, Vito," Borbola says, her thick eyebrow—basically a unibrow— scrunching together. "Who *are* you?"

He talks with his hands. "So I might-a be an old mob boss who took-a my family's fortune and went into hiding. And I might have just been found. But what of it? Nothin' to worry about, my dear." He pats her hand.

"What in the bloody hell is going on with them?" Ainsley asks no one in particular.

"I thought she had a husband in Russia," Frankie says.

"Ooh, *that's* him?!" Koemi crows, excitedly clapping her hands. "I thought I recognized his accent!"

"Shut up!" a bad guy yells. Then another smacks Vito with the butt of his gun. And torturing commences.

"Stop! Now!" Borbola tries. People scream and cry.

The robbers ignore everyone and focus on Vito. "Let's execute him on video call for the boss to see."

I look around at the team.

They're all looking to me. I clear my throat. "One last time?" They nod in agreement.

"Non, non, not me—no way," Remy says. "I am out of 'ere." He makes his way to the vault exit.

CHAPTER 16

The robbers move fast. One of them steps into Remy's path and jabs the barrel of his gun into his chest.

"I said everyone stays."

Remy scoffs. "You should not 'ave done zat." He lifts two fingers to his mouth and whistles loudly. It echoes sharply in the metal room. The robbers side-eye each other, confused.

There's a moment of silence, and then… a strange noise. Coming from everywhere at once. The ceiling. The inside of the walls. The floor, even. Everyone notices it, including the robbers.

"What the hell is that?" one of them grumbles angrily.

Then the insects appear. Having come from what must be every crack in the concrete, every pipe, every sewer grate on the block. Roaches and beetles flood into the vault like a massive school of fish. They coat the vault walls and floor—and the hostages. Then they just...

hold still, hundreds of tiny eyes focused on the perps.

Remy lifts his arms out by his sides. "I *said*, I am leaving," he tells the robbers threateningly. He waves his hands for the insects to charge.

But instead of doing so, they hesitate, side-eyeing him.

Hard.

"*No*," Remy says to them, paling as they appear to be communicating with him. "Do *not* bring *zat* up again."

A grasshopper lands on his collar and chirps twice.

Remy's face twists up and turns beet red with rage. "She was a three-year-old leetle girl! You wanted me to slap ze ice cream from her tiny hands so you could eat it? *Non!* I am not a monster!"

The insects seem unconvinced.

"Alright, enough of this!" a robber yells. He lifts his gun. So do the others. They take aim at Remy, and fire.

Time moves in slow motion. Instead of helping Remy and charging at the robbers or protecting him from the bullets now soaring through the air, they side-step, creating a wide berth around him so they aren't in the bullets' way.

Remy's eyes widen, and he opens his mouth to tell the bugs off just as the bullets rip into

his arms, legs, and side. He drops to the floor, clutching his bleeding limbs. "Vermin!" he groans out.

BWWWAAAAP.

A wretched, horrid smell fills the room. My eyes immediately go to the only possible culprit—Wekesa.

Sure enough, his eyes are wide. The gunfire startled him, so his power activated. The gas from his butt shoots through his turquoise pants, melting the butt of them wide open, and an awful green mist floats into the air. With every gun shot, Wakesa is startled and lets out more dangerous fumes. His butt is like a machine gun—an automatic machine butt. Yeah, that's it.

The robbers and hostages start gagging, coughing, clawing at their eyes.

"OH MY GOD," Koemi yells, animal-panic in her voice as she suddenly sprouts feathers.

"WHY IS IT IN MY MOUTH?! Wekesa, what did you eat?!"

"Uh... just some pre-dinner turkey finger sammies," he admits.

"What the hell is happening to you?!" a robber yells at her as she transforms partway into a large turkey. People squeal in horror.

"Bloody hell, Wakesa is going to kill us all." Ainsley mutters to the nearby teammates "We gotta get out of here, NOW!" Always with a flask ready, he starts chugging to activate his speed. He then bolts towards the exit, bouncing off people like a ball in a pinball game.

"*Guys*, we didn't even *try* to come up with a plan first!" I cry out.

Dejuan shakes his head when our eyes meet. "Typical," he says, shrugging.

"There's no *time* for a plan!" Koemi cries, gobbling loudly as her red wattle jiggles under her turkey beak. "Remy is going to *die*!"

CHAPTER 17

"Screw the money! We gotta jet, man! Or we're gonna die in here!" one of the robbers cries to his buddies.

"I don't think so!" Trish yells, dashing to the only exit of the vault and standing firmly before it. "Hey y'all!" she calls to us, her teammates, "keep the bad guys at bay! Everyone else, hurry up and get out of here! No pictures, please." She flips her hair—then accidentally breathes through her nose. The disgusting green mist fills her nostrils.

"No!" she squeals, gagging loudly. She tries to hold back, but Koemi vomits through her beak and lets out a horrible gobble-gag. The sound is so disturbing that Trish can't hold it in and vomits as well. It starts a chain reaction, everyone getting sick on each other, their eyes tearing from the gas. People panic and aimlessly bump into each other to find an exit through the thick smog. Ainsley is still bouncing around, creating more of a mosh pit than an escape. Remy is still badly bleeding on the ground, barely conscious, and barely visible in all the chaos. Vito and Borbola are huddled together, holding each other with their shirts pulled up over their noses.

"Anyone 'ave something to drink?" Borbola asks weakly. "I do not need to pee, so no muscles." Man, she *really* needs to drink more water. She's got one of the best gifts out of all of us and is *constantly* useless! Luckily, Ainsley's flask is on the ground near her. She grabs it and starts chugging like a champ.

"Move aside," a robber heaves through his hand, aiming his gun at Dejuan and me as we step in to block their path to Trish.

Dejuan cries out, startled by the weapon being pointed at his face, and out comes his green, blubbery form. Finally, he proves to be the only useful one of us. As a massive green blob, he takes up *a lot* of space. Sure, he's crushing some of the already injured hostages, but he's rolling toward the robbers, who have nowhere to run and eventually get trapped under him—flattened and stuck.

Trish can't take the smell. To avoid uncontrollable vomiting, she activates her power and turns to stone. The issue with this is her massive marble form is now completely blocking the only exit. Wekesa's mist can't escape. We're all trapped with it. Vomiting and blinded.

Eventually, *no one* is strong enough to endure it. Just as I start to strip down, it takes me under, too, my pants around my ankles, my shirt on the floor.

Thankfully, this is one of the few times when Trish's statue form doesn't last all night.

She's only marble for a maybe a half hour or so, not really sure, since I was unconscious. When she comes to, she stares around at the room of mostly unconscious individuals.

"Oh no!" she cries out, running to where Remy is nearly dead on the floor. She bends down, worried, and reaches for him.

Oh. Not him.

She sticks her hand in his jeans and pulls out his phone. She calls the number she memorized from the show producer's message, worried she's missed the pickup time. She's disoriented and has no clue how long she's been a statue and doesn't want to miss her chance at stardom.

A phone ringing loudly in the vault makes me stir slightly. My eyes still burn. I can barely make out Trish standing there on the phone, tapping an impatient foot in Remy's blood puddle, not even noticing it. She hears the ringing too, and turns to the now-dead robbers who had been crushed by Dejuan—who's now beside them on the ground, back to his normal form and unconscious from the gas.

Trish pulls the ringing phone out of one of the robber's pockets while keeping Remy's phone to her ear. She checks it, growls, and turns to her teammates.

"You *guys*!" she complains loudly. "Y'all *killed* one of my producers!"

"Hey, fam?" Wekesa croaks from by the now open doorway that no one's bothered to move through because they're too weak, "there's a camera in here. This whole mess has been caught on tape."

I slowly sit up and rub my sore eyes, my stomach still sick. Koemi lets out a massive fart.

I wouldn't be surprised if she just crapped herself again.

"Great," I say. The rest of my team seems to have come to—minus Remy. Though somehow, the insects have decided to give him aid and are collectively working together to patch up his bullet wounds. "You know what that means. First, let's drag these hostages outside before they wake up."

In the distance, I can hear sirens making their way toward us. The police.

CHAPTER 18

Remy is barely hanging on, the insects still saving his life as we climb back into the van. I drive us as fast as I can back to headquarters. Dejaun's watching YouTube videos to perform first aid on Remy.

Trish is on social media, scrolling. "The news spread fast," she says, showing us all the screen.

"Ew, I look *awful*!" Koemi cries, squinting at the small phone screen. She still has her turkey wattle, but everything else is back to normal. "When is this thing going to go away?!"

"That's the *least* of your problems," Borbola says, plugging her nose beside her. "You are covered in your own *feces*."

"Well *sorry* your mobster boyfriend doesn't have a toilet in his vault like everyone else!"

"Koemi, no one keeps toilets in their vault." "I would if I had one!" she whines.

"Yeah, because you're always needin' to take a dump!" Frankie says before he stuffs a bite of chocolate cake in his mouth.

Wekesa gapes at him.

"What?" Frankie asks defensively. "I had to try it. Not as good as my chocolate cake. No way, José." He sets it down.

"How can you even *think* about eating right now?" Dejuan asks, clutching his stomach and shaking his head.

Frankie shrugs.

"Has anyone figured out our identities yet?" I ask Trish from the driver's seat.

"Not yet."

"We're still gonna have to lay low for a while," Dejuan says.

"Figures," Frankie grumbles.

"Great," Wekesa mutters.

Borbola sighs heavily. I don't think we'll be seeing her smile again any time soon. I think I might prefer it that way.

"When will it be *my* time?" Trish asks herself.

"Urrghhhhh," Remy groans. A cricket chirps. "No, *you* should 'ave let me die. Now I

'ave to 'eer your incessant nagging."

When we get to headquarters, we all go inside and hurriedly gather everything we can, loading up the van again. It feels like just yesterday we were unloading it.

We have no choice. As superheroes, our identities cannot be discovered.

We have to leave.

"Where to now?" Koemi asks as we all climb back into the van with our possessions.

I feel a mix of emotions. On the one hand, I'm happy that it looks like we'll be a family for a little while longer. On the other...

It would have been really nice to go to college.

"What do you say we try something, coastal?" I ask.

The team grumbles their annoyed agreements.

CHAPTER 19

Our new headquarters is a dump.

Not in the metaphorical sense. An *actual* city dump. The air is thick with smog, flies buzz around, and somewhere nearby, I'm pretty sure two rats are in a cage match. The building we've squatted in might have been a former jail—long since abandoned and taken over by bugs (to Remy's disdain) and filth.

This sad, pathetic place is home.

Everyone's slouched in the main room, scattered across moldy chairs and stained sofas.

Except Frankie. He's still in the van, yelling his head off because we forgot to put the ramp down for his wheelchair. But we can't hear him. We don't even realize he's missing.

Koemi is staring blankly at a wall.

Ainsley's drunk, lying on the ground half asleep, one boot off.

Wekesa's patching the butt area of his jeans.

"I was gonna be a stuntman," Dejuan mutters, an arm over his face. "Now look where I am. Mom and Dad would be so proud. Not."

"I was going to be surrounded by loads of beautiful women," Ainsley mumbles as he pulls an old shower curtain over himself like a blanket. "Not loads of disgusting trash."

Borbola sips questionable-quality broth out of a cracked mug. "Vito said he call," she mutters, shaking her head.

"You all should 'ave put me out of my misery," Remy complains.

I sit on an overturned crate, my elbows on my knees, trying to breathe through the smell of rotten cabbage and depression. I look around at them—my team. My complete, dysfunctional, never-get-it-right team. They're exhausted. Gross. Barely holding it together.

And I was really gonna leave them.

But looking at them now—Koemi. Dejuan. Trish snoring with a piece of moldy bread, half-chewed, in her mouth...

They'd be lost without each other. Without... me. If I'm being honest, I'd be lost without them too.

The radio crackles. "Units respond. Fire at the apartment complex off 8th and Ellison. Civilians trapped on upper floors. Building is unstable." I sit upright.

"All units are currently engaged in a hostage incident downtown. We can't leave the scene. Call for backup in the next city over."

"Copy," someone replies. "They're over an hour away." We all glance around at each other.

"What?" Koemi whispers. She looks utterly clueless.

I hesitate. Then I stand. And, without breaking eye contact, I rip off my clothes.

"Aw, c'mon!" Dejuan groans.

Ainsley shields his eyes. "Every time!"

Koemi shrieks, hand to her mouth. "Aren't you embarrassed of that tiny thing?!" I stand tall, confident and unafraid, completely naked. "Let's go save some people." "Here we go," Wekesa groans.

I grin. "This time... we don't fail. I have a plan!", holding a finger in the air, smartness rushing through me like I've stepped into a warm bath.

And once again, the world's weirdest heroes rise:

Puddy Man.

Iron Granny.

Slosher Bolt.

Beasty Girl.

Green Mist.

Insect Lord.

Ms. Impassable

Flyin' Wheely.

And me...

Naked Worm.

We head for the door. We may be Super Useless. But we're trying super hard. Because if we don't...

Who else will?

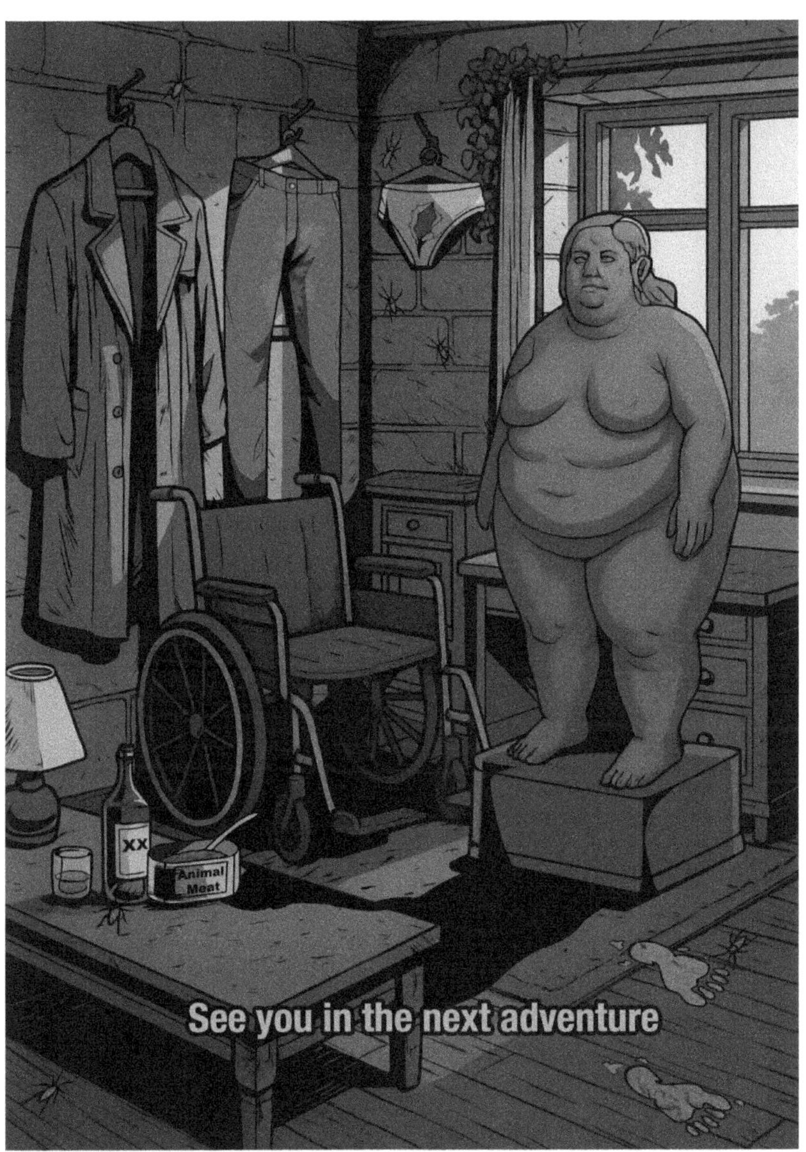
XX
Animal Meat
See you in the next adventure

While creating this story, I imagined endless crazy adventures these characters are bound to experience. I can't wait to share them with the world. It's gonna be fun!

- JM Lewis

Follow us and keep up to date on new releases!

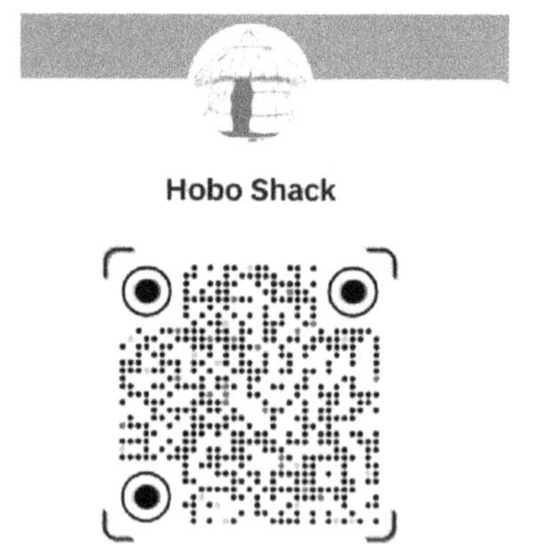

www.ingramcontent.com/pod-product-compliance
Lightning Source LLC
Chambersburg PA
CBHW061106100726
47911CB00012B/426

* 9 7 9 8 9 9 9 6 2 9 8 0 7 *